The Antique Store Cat

The Antique Store Cat

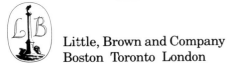

Little, Brown and Company
Boston Toronto London

Leslie Baker

To Grandma Freda and her seven dwarfs:
Hayley, Jamie, Peter, Michael, Laura, Kate, and Emma

First Edition

Library of Congress Cataloging-in-Publication Data
Baker, Leslie A.
  The antique store cat / Leslie Baker. — 1st ed.
    p.   cm.
  Summary: Alice, a calico cat, creates a stir when she makes an
"unauthorized" visit to an antique shop.
  ISBN 0-316-07837-9
  [1. Cats — Fiction.]   I. Title.
PZ7.B17435An   1992
[E] — dc20   90-29286

10 9 8 7 6 5 4 3 2 1

WOR

Published simultaneously in Canada
by Little, Brown & Company (Canada) Limited

Printed in the United States of America

On the morning of her birthday, Alice the cat tried yet again to escape from her third-story apartment. "No," Annie told her as she caught her squeezing through a window. Alice just licked her paws and stared out at the city streets below. For *no* meant nothing to Alice.

Later that day, as a birthday treat, Annie dressed Alice up and gave her a ride on the dumbwaiter. Alice went up and down several times. She was a good sport at first. But after the seventh ride she decided enough was enough. She got off in the cellar and escaped through a broken window.

Alice was glad to be outside. The fall wind blew hundreds of golden leaves from the trees. Just for fun, she chased a few. Then, without warning, it began to rain heavily. Racing up the sidewalk, Alice searched for her home. But all the doors looked the same. Which one was hers?

Eventually she found shelter in the doorway of a shop. Wet and cold, Alice meowed pitifully. Soon the door opened, and she heard a kind voice. Looking up, Alice saw an old man smiling at her. She was too miserable to protest when he carried her inside.

While the man dried her off, Alice glanced around. The store
was filled top to bottom with all kinds of things. Furniture,
knickknacks, trinkets, and toys, all covered with a bit of dust,
were piled everywhere.

Alice couldn't wait to investigate. Jumping into a box, she tiptoed through some glass bottles. "No, no!" cried the old man. But *no* meant nothing to Alice. She continued her exploration, stopping now and then to sniff something of interest. Just as the man was about to scoop her into his arms, the bell over the door tinkled. Someone walked in.

Alice couldn't believe her eyes. In front of her stood a grim-faced woman with a statue in her arms and a large bird on her shoulders. *"Cat!"* shrieked the bird. Alice's heart beat faster. This bird talked!

Curious, Alice wanted a closer look. Crouching low, she moved slowly and steadily toward the bird. Meanwhile, the woman tried to sell the statue to the old man. They were so busy that neither one saw Alice eagerly twitching her tail at the bird. Finally, unable to resist any longer, Alice prepared to pounce. The terrified bird squawked, *"No, no, no!"*

But *no* meant nothing to Alice. In a flash she slid across the
counter, sending the bird into the air and the statue to the floor,
where it smashed into a million pieces.

The woman shook her fists as Alice ran for cover. "You'll pay
for this!" she yelled at the old man, who covered his face with his
hands. Alice came out and rubbed herself against her sad friend's
legs. Then, to amuse herself, she began to play with the broken
statue. "No," the downhearted man told Alice.

But *no* meant nothing to Alice. She cheerfully continued her game. As she turned one of the pieces over with her paw, the old man suddenly took notice. He picked up a small part and studied it carefully. "This is a fake," he said to the woman. "Fake!" echoed the bird as it flew out the door. "I told you never to say that!" yelled the woman as she ran after it.

The old man hugged Alice. "You saved the day, my little antique store cat," he said. He placed her in the window of his shop. From her new perch she could see up and down the sidewalk. It was interesting, but she missed the view from her apartment high above the city streets. Her growling stomach reminded her she missed her dinner as well.

Then Alice heard a familiar tap-tap-tapping. She looked out of the window excitedly. Annie was walking down the street banging on Alice's food bowl and calling out her name. Under her arm she carried a birthday present. Alice raced out of the shop toward Annie.

While Alice ate her dinner, Annie opened the present. Inside
was a new collar and leash for Alice. "Now we can escape from
the apartment together," Annie whispered to her cat. She snapped
the leash on Alice. But Alice had other ideas. After two steps she
stopped short. "No," Annie scolded her cat. But Alice just sat on
the pavement and licked her paws.

For *no* meant nothing to Alice.